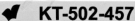

BEST WISHES...

For the wolves.

With thanks to Paula Wiseman and Victoria Rock,
and to Barry Lopez, who walked there before me. – J.L.

To: Tex, Diane, Tom, and Sasha...dedicated friends
of the wolf. – J.V.Z.

Text copyright © 1993 Jonathan London.
Illustrations copyright © 1993 Jon Van Zyle.
All rights reserved.
Book design by Carrie Leeb.
Printed in Hong Kong.

Library of Congress Cataloging-in-Publication Data

London, Jonathan, 1947-
The eyes of Gray Wolf / by Jonathan London;
illustrated by Jon Van Zyle.
p. cm.
Summary: On a cold northern night,
a restless gray wolf encounters an
unknown wolf pack, from which a
young white wolf steps out and
they become mates.
ISBN 0-8118-0285-X :
1. Wolves–Juvenile fiction.
[1. Wolves–Fiction.] I. Van
Zyle, Jon, ill. II. Title.
PZ10.3.L8534Ey 1993
[E]–dc20   92-35987
                    CIP
                    AC

Distributed in Canada
by Raincoast Books
112 East Third Avenue
Vancouver, B.C. V5T 1C8

10 9 8 7 6 5 4 3 2 1

Chronicle Books
275 Fifth Street
San Francisco, California 94103

THE EYES OF GRAY WOLF

by Jonathan London

illustrated by Jon Van Zyle

Chronicle Books · San Francisco

As the full moon rises in the winter sky,
Gray Wolf goes hunting. He is restless.
He has lost his mate to a man's steel trap.

The northern night is cold and still.
Gray Wolf floats over the snow, drifting
through the woods, flowing like water.

He pauses only to inspect a scent mark,
or to claim his territory with his own scent.
He paws among rocks, where a year ago
he had hidden some meat—raided long since
by eagles, weasels, or wolverines.

Gray Wolf leaps a frozen creek and
climbs along the spine of a low ridge.

At the top, he closes his eyes, throws back his head, and howls. A wild, untamed music, it seems to bounce off the moon, echoing from the mountains and filling the gullies and valleys.

Nose into the wind, he returns to the
hunt. In a moon-bright forest clearing,
he flushes a snowshoe hare.

Shadows bound across the sparkling snow.
Hare is no match for Gray Wolf.

But Gray Wolf comes to a halt, letting Hare flee. He sniffs the crisp night air, sensing danger. The fur on his neck stands up. There in the shadows he sees a wolf pack.

Poised, absolutely still, Gray Wolf stands alone and stares. His eyes burn like steady flames.

The leader of the pack stares back. Their eyes
lock. The moon burns a hole in the night.

Suddenly a young white wolf, brilliant as the moonlight, steps out from the pack.

And the pack, still as stone,
watches as Gray Wolf and
White Wolf circle each other.
Even the trees seem to
hold their breath.

At the edge of the meadow they begin,
at the exact same moment, to wag
their tails and lope off across the snow,
their heads held high. The trees breathe
as the two wolves rise into the hills.

When they curl up together,
White Wolf buries her nose beneath
her bushy tail and goes to sleep.
But Gray Wolf's eyes remain open.
It has been a long night.
The moon has crossed the sky.
As it sinks in the west, the eyes
of Gray Wolf become twin moons.

In the spring the two wolves will start a new pack of their own.

What You Can Do To Help

There are many groups working to preserve the majestic wolf and to reintroduce wolves into their native habitats. If you would like more information, or if you would like to help, you can contact any one of the following organizations.

INTERNATIONAL WOLF CENTER
c/o Vermilion Community College
1900 East Camp Street
Ely, MN 55731

H.O.W.L. (Help Our Wolves Live)
4600 Emerson Avenue South
Minneapolis, MN 55409

WOLF HAVEN
3111 Offut Lake Road
Tenino, WA 98589

DEFENDERS OF WILDLIFE
1244 19th Street NW
Washington, D.C. 20036

CANADIAN WOLF DEFENDERS
P.O. Box 3480 Station D
Edmonton, Alberta
Canada T5L 4J3

WOLF!
P.O. Box 112
Clifton Heights, PA 19018

WOLF RIDGE ENVIRONMENTAL
LEARNING CENTER
230 Cranberry Road
Finland, MN 55603
(218) 353-7414

WOLF SONG OF ALASKA
6430 Ridge Tree Circle
Anchorage, AK 99516
(907) 274-9653 or (907) 346-1345

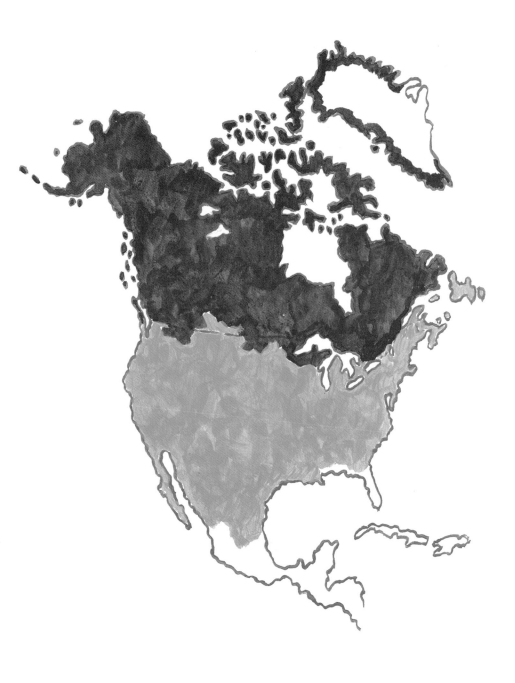

 The wolf's range in the 1700s

 The wolf's range today

A Note from the Author

The Lakota Sioux call the wolf *shunk-manitu tanka*: "the animal who looks like a dog, but is a powerful spirit." This wild ancestor of the dog is a master hunter, and traditionally the Lakota people, among other Northern Plains Indians, learned from wolves how to hunt, and how to survive the long, cold winters. A wolf pack is similar to a human family, usually with a mother and father wolf as leaders, followed by uncles and aunts, brothers and sisters. The mother and father, who generally mate for life, lead the hunt, and defend the young from bears and their territory from other packs. The wolves hunt and play together, and care for each other.

Long ago, the wild howls of wolves were heard all across the Northern Hemisphere, throughout Europe and northern Asia as well as all of North America. But in the last few hundred years, humans have declared war on wolves, fearing them instead of learning from them — and learning how to live with them. In reality, wolves tend to be shy and try to avoid people, yet since the Middle Ages wolves have been seen as terrifying and evil. In the late 19th and early 20th centuries, an attempt was made in North America to systematically destroy them. During this time, wolves were brutally hunted and poisoned to the brink of extinction.

Today, in the United States, wolves are endangered in the lower 48 states, except for Minnesota, where they are threatened. Thousands still roam Alaska and Canada, and conservationists are trying to protect wolves wandering back across the border to their ancestral homes in Montana, Idaho and Washington. Hopes are strong for a plan to reintroduce wolves to the Yellowstone National Park and elsewhere in the U.S. In western Europe, wolves survive in small numbers in the mountainous regions of Spain, Greece, Portugal, Italy and Scandinavia, while in eastern Europe, Siberia and the rest of Asia, nobody knows how many wolves remain. If we listen carefully, will we again hear "the wild, untamed music" of the wolves? By learning about wolves and their environment, and supporting organizations and sanctuaries which seek to protect the wolves, the answer could be "yes."